Sleepytime
PLAYSONGS

Baby's restful day in songs and pictures

D0511175

Compiled by **Sheena Roberts**

Illustrated by **Rachel Fuller**

Performed by **Sandra Kerr, Leon Rosselson** and **Janet Russell**

A & C BLACK · LONDON in association with PLAYSONGS PUBLICATIO

Sleepy dreams, sleepy head ~

time to leave
your sleepy bed

Last night as I lay sleeping

Little babies+
A dance song ~ perfect for rocking baby in your arms as you move to the lilting rhythm.

Bigger babies+
Sweep him up from his cot and 'fly' him round with you.

Land him smoothly back into his cot or onto his play mat.

Sleepy little baby

Little babies+
Ease baby into wakefulness by drawing attention to sounds he likes. Each time you sing, make a new sound: shake a favourite rattle, clap your hands, or hum the melody.

Take his hands and rock him from side to side as he lies on his back in his cot or on his changing mat.

Make a sound to one side of him then to the other. He'll soon be turning his head towards it.

Last night as I lay sleeping

1

Last night as I lay sleeping,
I dreamt that I was sailing
To the Isle of Man in a frying pan
And back again by morning.

Last night as I lay sleeping,
I dreamt that I was flying
To the Isle of Skye on an apple pie,
And back again by morning.

Last night as I lay sleeping,
I dreamt that I was gliding
To the Isle of Mull on a herring gull,
And back again by morning.

Sleepy little baby

2

Sleepy little baby,
You have had your rest,
Listen to the sounds around
That you like best.

Listen to the east ~
Listen to the west ~
Listen to the sounds around
That you like best.

Oh moon ~ play with me 3

Oh moon, would you come and play with me today?
Oh moon, would you come and play with me today?
Would you bring your golden boat
And take me far away?

New day 4

When a new day's begun, up with the yellow sun,
We'll say hello to the start of a working day,
Then when I have to go, give me a hug
And I'll say, baby, goodbye, my baby, bye bye.

I'll say goodbye to you, you'll say goodbye to me,
We'll say hello to all the friends that we meet today,
Then even though I'm gone, the day won't be very long,
My baby, don't cry, my baby, don't cry.

Then when the day is gone and all my work is done,
I'll come right home to you, kiss you and cuddle you,
You'll play a game with me, I'll play a game with you,
My baby, hi, baby, my baby, hi, baby, hi!

while you're on the changing mat

Baby Michael

Baby Michael

Little babies+
- A peekaboo song to gain a fractious baby's attention and earn you smiles.
- Peek from behind a scarf or cover him lightly with it. He will soon enjoy pulling it off himself.

Toddlers+
- Sing this as a hide and seek game.
- When your toddler has found a hiding place, sing through all the possible places he might be until you spot him and sing 'I see you...'

Baby Michael 5

- Baby Michael, Baby Michael,
  Where are you, where are you?
- Lying on your changing mat,
  Lying on your changing mat,
  I see you,
  Yes I do!

Under teddy's jumper

Under teddy's jumper

Little babies+
- Pat baby's tummy to the beat of the rhyme.
- 'Squeak' baby's tummy.

Bigger babies+
- He will have fun locating his own tummy button as you say the rhyme.

Under teddy's jumper 6

- Under teddy's jumper,
  Under teddy's vest,
  There's a little button,
  Waiting to be pressed.
  Lift up teddy's jumper,
  Take a little peek ~
- Press the little button,
  Make him squeak, squeak, squeak!

Slowly slowly 7

Slowly slowly, very slowly
Creeps the garden snail,
Slowly slowly, very slowly
Up the wooden rail.

Quickly quickly, very quickly
Runs the little mouse,
Quickly quickly, very quickly
Round about the house.

Shoe a little horse 8

Shoe a little horse,
Shoe a little mare,
But let the little colt
Go bare, bare, bare.

On my knee, up you jump –
Bounce along and down you bump

The gypsy rover

Little babies+
Play while he's lying on his changing mat or on your legs.

● Walk your fingers up his body and tickle his nose, cheek, chin...

■ Take his hands and rock him.

Bigger babies+
● Sit him on your knee facing outwards.

Walk your fingers over his shoulders and down to his toes, then tickle his nose, stroke his cheek, blow him a kiss...

■ Sway him from side to side on your knee.

Jackass with him long tail

Little babies+
● A rocking song.

Bigger babies+
● Swing him from side to side on your knee at a slow relaxed pace.

■ Bounce him at the double, for a playful contrast.

The gypsy rover

9

● The gypsy rover came over the hill,
Down in the valley so shady,
He whistled and he sang
Till the green woods rang,
And he tickled the nose of a baby.

■ Ah dee doo, ah dee doo da day...

10

Jackass with him long tail

● Jackass with him long tail,
Bag a coco comin down.
Jackass with him long tail,
Bag a coco comin down.
■ No tease him, no worry him,
No make the hamper squeeze him.
Jackass with him long tail,
Bag a coco comin down.

Jackass with him long tail,
Bag a minty comin down.
Jackass with him long tail,
Bag a minty comin down.
No threaten him, no beat him,
No make them boy maltreat him.
Jackass with him long tail,
Bag a minty comin down.

Jackass with him long tail,
Bag a yampi comin down.
Jackass with him long tail,
Bag a yampi comin down.
No ride him, no hackle him,
No make gingi-fly tackle him.
Jackass with him long tail,
Bag a yampi comin down.

Trot trot trot 11

Trot trot trot,
Go and never stop,
Take me safe, my little pony,
Though the way is
Rough and stony,
Go and never stop,
Trot trot trot trot trot.

Jump jump jump,
Come down with a bump,
Take me safe, my little pony,
Though the way is
Rough and stony,
Jump jump jump,
Come down with a bump.

The mocking bird song 12

Hush, little baby, don't say a word,
Daddy's going to buy you
    a mocking bird.

And if that mocking bird don't sing,
Daddy's going to buy you
    a diamond ring.

And if that diamond ring turns brass,
Daddy's going to buy you
    a looking glass.

And if that looking glass gets broke,
Daddy's going to buy you
    a billy goat.

And if that billy goat won't pull,
Daddy's going to buy you
    a cart and bull.

And if that cart and bull turns over,
Daddy's going to buy you
    a dog named Rover.

And if that dog named Rover
    won't bark,
Daddy's going to buy you
    a horse and cart.

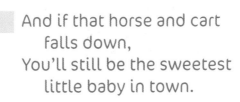

And if that horse and cart
    falls down,
You'll still be the sweetest
    little baby in town.

Trot trot trot

Little babies+
Take little jogging steps with him in your arms so he feels the beat.

Bigger babies+
A fast knee bouncer with extra high bounces on 'jump'.

Toddlers+
He will enjoy trotting and jumping on his own to this: a good one for him to feel in his whole body the difference in pace.

The mocking bird song

Little babies+
A rocking lullaby.

Bigger babies+
Cross your leg over your knee, and hold his hands as he sits astride your ankle. Swing him gently to the slow beat.

Swing him down to the floor, then right up into your lap for a cuddle.

Jingle, ring, tippy tap ~
time to take a midday nap

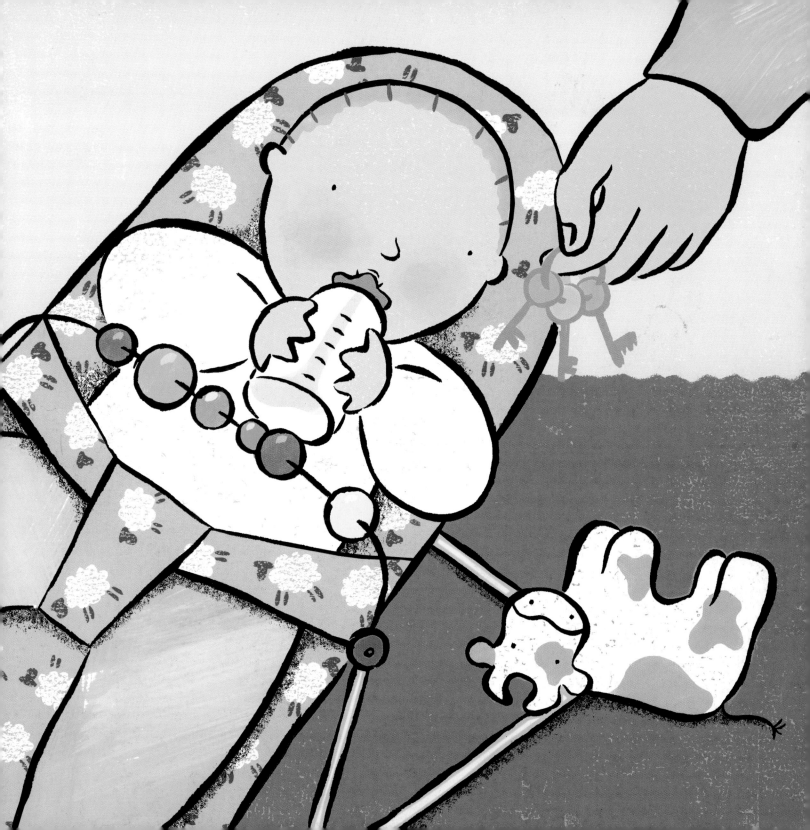

Jingle jangle

Little babies+

Use any object that makes an interesting but soothing sound to capture his attention and calm him when he has reached that difficult, over-tired state of just needing sleep.

- Make sounds with anything interesting to hand: a bunch of keys, a string of beads, a couple of spoons, some rustly paper ~ or simply hum to him...

- Move the sound object around, making long or short sounds with it, or keeping the beat.

Hush a baw birdie, croon

Little babies+

- This Scottish croon has the perfect pace for comforting and relaxing a crying baby. It is the combination of movement and rhythmical sound which makes a croon so effective.

Jingle jangle 13

Jingle jangle go the keys,
Can you hear the sound?
Jingle jangle go the keys,
Hear it all around.

Hear the sound around your ears,
And hear it near your feet,
First it makes a long, long sound
And then it keeps the beat,
    beat, beat, beat.

Rattle rattle go the beads,
Can you hear the sound?
Rattle rattle go the beads,
Hear it all around.

Hear the sound around your ears...

Tappy tappy go the spoons,
Can you hear the sound?
Tappy tappy go the spoons,
Hear it all around.

Hear the sound around your ears,
And hear it near your feet,
First they make so many sounds
And then they keep the beat,
    beat, beat, beat.

Hush a baw birdie, croon 14

Hush a baw birdie, croon croon,
Hush a baw birdie, croon.
The sheep are gane to the mountain top
And they'll nay be hame till noon, noon.
And it's braw milking the kye, kye,
And it's braw milking the kye,
The bells are ringing, the birds are singing,
The wild deer come galloping by, by.
Hush a baw birdie, croon croon,
Hush a baw birdie, croon.

Bee-o bee-o

● Bee-o, bee-o, bonny bonny bee-o,
Bee-o, bee-o, bonny babe o' mine.
Bee-o, bee-o, bonny bonny bee-o,
Bee-o, bee-o, bonny babe o' mine.

■ I love my little baby without a doubt or maybe,
I love you, I love you, I love you 'cos you're mine.
I love my little baby without a doubt or maybe,
I love you, I love you, I love you 'cos you're mine.

Bee-o, bee-o, bonny bonny bee-o...

I love my little baby without a doubt or maybe,
I love you all from tip to toe, I love you 'cos you're mine.
I love my little baby without a doubt or maybe,
I love you all from tip to toe, I love you 'cos you're mine.

Bee-o, bee-o, bonny bonny bee-o...

Bee-o bee-o

Little babies+
This croon is wonderful not only for daytime comforting, but also for helping you both through a wakeful night. Its gentle, mesmeric lilt is guaranteed to calm you, as well as your baby, during a stressful time.

● Pat or smooth your hand over baby's back as you move to the steady rhythm.

■ Make the song even more special by singing your child's own name at 'I love my little...'

Not a tick, not a chime

– in our dandelion time

Listening walk

Little babies+
Point to and say the names and sounds of the things you see and hear together, whether you are out of doors or sitting quietly looking at the pictures in this book.

Make up verses of your own.

Wiggle worm

Little babies+
Wiggle your finger up baby's body and tickle his chin.

Toddlers+
This is a lovely one for your toddler to play with a younger sibling ~ or with you.

Incy wincy spider

Little babies+
Cradle baby in one arm. Walk your fingers up him, then run them down.

Draw a big semicircle with baby's hand. Walk your fingers back up him again.

Toddlers+
Encourage him to do the actions himself.

Listening walk 16

Mummy took me out for a walk today,
We saw such exciting things on the way.
'Look! My love! Dog,' says Mum,
'Dog,' I say. 'Yes, dog,' says Mum,
  'Ruff ruff ruff ruff ruff ruff.'

Granny took me out for a walk today,
We saw such exciting things on the way.
'Look! My love! Car,' says Gran,
'Car,' I say. 'Yes, car,' says Gran,
  'Vroom vroom vroom vroom vroom vroom.'

Daddy took me out for a walk today,
We saw such exciting things on the way.
'Look! My love! Bee,' says Dad,
'Bee,' I say. 'Yes, bee,' says Dad,
  'Buzza buzza buzz buzz ~ buzz.'

Wiggle worm 17

Here comes a little
Wiggle worm,
  Wiggle,
  Wiggle,
  Wiggle.
He wiggles up the
Drainpipe ~
And makes the baby
  Giggle!

Incy wincy spider 18

Incy wincy spider climbed the water spout,
Down came the rain and washed the spider out,

Out came the sun and dried up all the rain,
Incy wincy spider climbed the spout again.

Dandelion clock 19

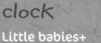

What shall we do with the dandelion green?
We could make a gift for a flower fairy queen,
Or tell her the time by the silent chime,
No tick no tock, of the dandelion clock, just,
   Puff ~ one o'clock, puff ~ two o'clock,
   Puff ~ three o'clock.

What shall we do with the dandelion down?
For a fairy queen we could make a little crown,
Or tell her the time by the silent chime,
No tick no tock, of the dandelion clock, just,
   Puff ~ four o'clock, puff ~ five o'clock,
   Puff ~ six o'clock.

What shall we do with the dandelion seeds?
For a fairy queen we could make a string of beads,
Or tell her the time by the silent chime,
No tick no tock, of the dandelion clock, just,
   Puff ~ seven o'clock, puff ~ eight o'clock,
   Puff ~ nine o'clock.

What shall we do with the dandelion head?
For a fairy queen we could make a cosy bed,
Or tell her the time by the silent chime,
No tick no tock, of the dandelion clock, just,
   Puff ~ ten o'clock, puff ~ eleven o'clock,
   Puff ~ twelve o'clock.

Dandelion clock

Little babies+
Rock him in your arms then blow lightly on his face on each 'puff'.

Bigger babies+
Perform these actions as you sing with him resting against your raised knees. As he grows in confidence, he will join in more and more:

'dandelion green' ~ loosely cup hands into a ball;

'little crown' ~ fingers pointing upwards, hands on head;

'bed' ~ rock cupped palms;

'string of beads' ~ hold the ends of pretend beads between index fingers and thumbs;

wag finger from side to side;

blow hands open on each 'puff'.

Toddlers+
Encourage him to copy you as you indicate a count of three with your fingers.

Here's a splish and a splosh ~

and a sponge for a wash

Underneath the water

Underneath the water

Little babies+

● Support baby facing you on your raised knees. Cup his hands in yours and swish them around. Lower your knees, and baby with them, on 'tea'.

■ Swish hands again then raise your knees and pull his hands to bring him back up to sitting.

Bigger babies+

● Hold baby firmly in your arms as you stand and sway (this can be done from a chair if it's easier).

■ Double yourself over so that he turns upside down on 'for my tea'.

Turn yourselves back upright on 'can't catch me'.

Splish splash splosh

Little babies+

● 'Sponge' feet, knees, tum, shoulders up to head, then back down to feet ~ in the rhythm of the song.

Underneath the water

● Underneath the water,
Underneath the sea,
Catching fishes
For my tea.

■ Swimming in the water,
Swimming in the sea,
All the little fishes
They can't catch me.

20

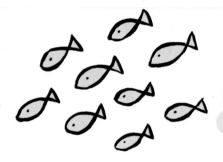

Splish splash splosh

● Splish splash splosh,
What are we going to wash?
Down the street
Wash our feet,
Climb the trees
Wash our knees,
Round the park
And wash our tum,
Up the hill
And down we come,
Splish splash splosh.

21

Dance to your daddy

Dance to your daddy
Sing to your mammy,
Dance to your daddy
To your mammy sing.

You shall have a fishy
On a little dishy,
You shall have a mackerel
When the boat comes in.

Yonder comes your mither,
She's a canny woman,
Yonder comes your father,
He's a canny man.
    Dance to your daddy...

You shall have a fishy
On a little dishy
You shall have a herrin'
When the boat comes in.

May we have whor milk
Cos oft we stand in need,
And weel made the keel
That brings the bairns their bread.
    Dance to your daddy...

You shall have a fishy
On a little dishy
You shall have a salmon
When the boat comes in.

Bubble

Here's the soap
To wash your hands,
Blow a big bubble ~
Fooooooooooo,
And see where it lands ~

Pop!

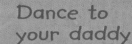

Dance to your daddy

Little babies+
Sing while towelling baby dry after his bath and whenever you want a happy, dancing song to amuse him.

Bigger babies+
Use anytime as a knee-bouncer or ankle-rider ~ cross your leg, hold baby's hands firmly, and sit him astride your swinging ankle.

Bubble

Little babies+
Blow a pretend bubble, then trace its path in the air with a fingertip.

'Pop' the 'bubble' on any part of baby ~ nose, cheek, toes, tummy, ear...

Play any of these bath time songs or rhymes with a real sponge, soap and bubbles while bathing him.

With my hand

round the shape of your face

I can trace ~

Face trace

Face trace

Little babies+

Gently touch or stroke each part of baby's face and take his hand to help him touch yours during this intimate conversation song.

Even the tiniest baby will love the direct eye contact you have with him, and the pleasure of your undivided attention.

Bigger babies+

Continue using the song in the same way as for a little baby.

As he gets older he will enjoy the concept of 'yours' and 'mine' more and more, and he will absorb the names and positions of features at the same time.

Face trace 24

I'll tap your chin to see if you're in,
You can tap mine, that will be fine,
Yours, mine, that will be fine.

I'll touch your mouth, from north down to south,
You can touch mine, that will be fine,
Yours, mine, that will be fine.

I'll beep your nose, that sniffles and blows,
You can beep mine, that will be fine,
Yours, mine, that will be fine.

I'll pat your cheeks for kisses and tweaks,
You can pat mine, that will be fine,
Yours, mine, that will be fine.

I'll kiss your eyes, wide as the skies,
You can kiss mine, that will be fine,
Yours, mine, that will be fine.

I'll tickle your ear, one there, one here,
You tickle mine, that will be fine,
Yours, mine, that will be fine.

Now I have traced the shape of your face,
You have traced mine, wasn't that fine?
Yours, mine, wasn't that fine?

Lavender's blue

Lavender's blue, dilly dilly,
Lavender's green;
When I am king, dilly dilly,
You shall be queen.

Who told you so, dilly dilly,
Who told you so?
'Twas mine own heart, dilly dilly,
That told me so.

Call up your men, dilly dilly,
Set them to work,
Some to the plough, dilly dilly,
Some to the fork.

Some to make hay, dilly dilly,
Some to reap corn,
Whilst you and I, dilly dilly,
Keep ourselves warm.

Roses are red, dilly dilly,
Violets are blue;
You will love me, dilly dilly,
I will love you.

Let the birds sing, dilly dilly,
Let the lambs play;
We shall be safe, dilly dilly,
Out of harm's way.

Mousey Brown

Up the tall white
candlestick
went
Little Mousey Brown.

He blew the candle
out ~
PUFF!
And then he ran
right
down.

Souallé

Souallé, souallé, souallé, souallé,
Souallé, souallé, souallé, souallé.

Lavender's blue

Little babies+
A song like this or like Souallé below is perfect for sessions of whole body massage. The even, slow pace suits the stroke of your hand as you work a little natural oil into his skin*.

* For guidance on massage and the use of oils, refer to a good text book, a health visitor or qualified masseur.

Mousey Brown

Little babies+
Use firm strokes or circling movements with the flat of your hand, working up baby's arm from shoulder to hand as you say the rhyme. Blow lightly on baby's hand and slide your hand smoothly back to his shoulder.

Souallé

Little babies+
Use for whole body massage in the same way as Lavender's blue.

Not a peep, count sheep ~

...hush a bye...
go to sleep...

Dad's lullaby 28

On my shoulder lay your head,
You're the best little baby
   a body ever had,
Time I was with your mam in bed,
Not a peep, count sheep,
Go to sleep for your dad.

Your mam's your comfort
   all day through,
You're the best little baby
   a body ever had,
It's my turn now to care for you,
Not a peep, count sheep,
Go to sleep for your dad.

I'm glad you came and you're
   here to stay,
You're the best little baby
   a body ever had,
But I'm up for work at the
   break of day,
Not a peep, count sheep,
Go to sleep for your dad.

On my shoulder lay your head,
You're the best little baby
   a body ever had,
Time I was with your mam in bed,
Not a peep, count sheep,
Go to sleep for your dad.

Dad's lullaby
Hush a bye,
baby bye

All
The first song is a
new lullaby with a
Northumberland
setting, the second
is an old North
American song which
is sung here as a
round.

Hush a bye, baby bye 29

Hush a bye, baby bye,
Hush a bye, baby bye,
Mumma's gone to the mailboat,
Mumma's gone to the mailboat...

Bye-o, baby, bye, bye,
Bye-o, baby, bye, bye...
Bye,
Bye...